H MAN 2 : THE BATTLE OF CARDINAL (ENGLISH)

SUMEET KUMAR

Sumeet Kumar

Sumeet Kumar , A adult who experiences many phases of life , a well known writer and a writer of new era . In reality he is a writter as well as singer (as a hobby) and a standup comedian . Very exciting and interesting fact about him is that he is author of New era i.e. he starts his journey of writing at the age when he was going to schools to get the study . His streak of 100 books will be the great achievement for him in future. His some famous works i.e. Maturity Of Love (Genre - Love),Privacy For Dream (Genre

- Middle Class), Army Squad ofLove (Genre- The Seperation of Army Love), 5 Days of Love(Genre- Temporarily Love), Th e Endearment Of Love(Genre - Historical Era Of Love), Social Destruction Indo-Pak (Genre - The Story of The Love At The Time Of Division Of India And Pakistan), Middle Class Soul (Genre - The Dreams of Middle Class), The Accursed Kanatpur (Genre -The Horrific Story Of A Village), Wrong Number (Genre -The Suspenseful Physco Killer Story), The Secrecy OfDeadly Midnight (Genre - The Suspense About a Crime),Fragile Religious Of Death (Genre- The Death Of A TrustfulPerson), Nature Vs Science (Genre - The Future Battle Between Nature And Science In A Horrific Way), Generic Man (Genre - The Dream of I.I.T), The Unconsious 12 Hours(Genre - The Illusion At Stage Of Comma), The StrangeBurden (Genre - The Burden Of Love) , Her Existence (Genre- The Female Pain In The Society) , Jockstrap Prize (Genre -The True Story Of A National Athlete) , H Man [Hindi] (Genre - Superhero Tragic Story), H Man [English] (Genre - Superhero Tragic Story) , Maturity Of Love [Englsih] (Genre - Love) and many more are available on various geners on the offcial platform of **Amazon, Flipkart and Notionpress**. You can buy them from there.

Contents

Acknowledgements

Aman Kumar

Special Thanks to **Aman Kumar** who worked so hard in the preparation of this book. He has continually put with my passive voice, omission of words, and late night calls. You have been wonderful. Thanks to him for his precious time in reviewing proposals , individual chapters and early drafts, along with his suggestions on the applicability of the material to the world.

I

FREEDOM IN SKY

Today I am going to start such a story, whose story is not only a fact, but it is the knowledge in which many people had given their lives in the pond, that too the foot was the thing to get it, what was the most wonderful thing in the universe, which will be mentioned further. I am going to say syedush raiyat seh every single witness is not aware of it at all because it is a matter of time when the thinking of human race was far from it, some dreams would have come true, whose glimpse is visible in front It is possible that there are different types of powers in the world and they can be used properly only where there is the foundation of humanity, where the human race is with each other very kindly. There are many more, in whose shadow, many logs were trying to call themselves protected, that in the beginning it is not necessary that every single device can try to move forward with your thinking.

Many do not take them after you, when we think of the world to do something, then its limits would be very different from us. Thoughts try to throw us in many different directions and even though we have been told to separate them, yet we have no say in one thing, which we can never say to separate ourselves from ourselves, time Changing feet can change the way, feet can change the way of the floor I am trying to show every direction a bash rake, which is probably my destination, it is very difficult, the feet are probably near someone's destination, when I earth 59 feet, then my thinking also became like a human race, due to which I used to try to run away, I kept myself safe from their friends. The shadow of my past has told me to separate myself too, which started where my parents tried to end it What I am writing, I may be lacking in my share, maybe not stay in the future, yet my friends who are related to Earth 59, may not share them with their friends. I can't separate today, if Uncle Lucifer was with me, I would tell him those all word and a kind of pain , which I feel Master Yang Lu had said that we can protect our feelings only as long as we are angry with us.

He had also said to me that emotion always works to make a person wander from his path and even if we leave the time, it would have left us, then move forward towards your destination and do something good, with your feelings only. Look at the ruin of your future, maybe they were right, the feelings of a man's mother give seh murder on every side, when the earth is 59 feet, then I found such a wonderful thing that only the lovers get it What I was doing after all, the shadow of my past has become in my mind, feeling strange right bail, I have lost myself in my eyes, I have fallen in love with those feelings, which I have been taught to keep me from my destination all the time. I am saying that I have forgotten to go away, I am missing my planet a lot today, I always thought that those who I myself say more, when I go ahead I will see the pain of my enemy, why do I not understand why and for whom it is not understood in the batis, even if I die today, it will be my victory in this, I can never go against my masters. The world I hated, I lost every nib of my childhood, is it still with me, I have given up that destination I am different, my thoughts are different, my feelings are different and they do not know anything about my powers My real parents are not the feet, even if they were, they would not have got so much love since childhood, we were only taught how to defend ourselves: how we fight, how to defeat our enemies in battle, the feet of this morning are not completely different nor Neither any training, nor strict rules nor operation, it is not such a thing that it does not remember its sapta planet, Miss Haget, Miss Faret Yet doesn't remember her squad, if time's Gujar Singh supported me, then maybe for some time and I say to be alone in this journey, I say to build relationships in the real world of my dad and mom I love my powers, my feet, not more than that, people are totally different, their thoughts are totally different, it's just the four walls of happiness that make my every morning colorful, Uncle Stub, whom I call dad, he makes me ahhi all the time Keep asking you where did you eat food and I tell them all the time that I have eaten and every night Aunt Gavier listens to me a new story that in the universe there was holy of god and type of composition, even if I leave everyone behind.

So how olive my feelings have become hubby on me today, I don't understand, I tell myself that hard work can never be lucky, maybe for the first time today I feel that the master was wrong too It is luck that if my luck is not bigger than my efforts, then I may never come to my mother and grandfather's residental house known , what is the line of life, what is the importance of this, I have come to the world to know that the world that hated the body, misunderstood the people, after all, he only told the reason for love, the reason why I never stood apart from those souls. Didn't understand when my canda ship collided with Asteriodes, whose name was Python, then maybe that reason was not enough to send me this because it was a real enmity which was created by my own new when my canda ship was protected by time protection. Earth 59 feet landed straight in the collision, my condition was not quite right at the time, I was completely engulfed in flames, why did I not die? I was in a world where my dad was born, I didn't even know at that time that the planet foot I am is some other Earth 59, it came to my feet, how I can't even remember anything right at that time I didn't remember my squad, nor do I know which cell to belong Nor did my family, who were the feet of the planet planet, felt that a new life was born inside me, it was different from the walls and many things, that even the Atmosphere could not emerge from the disciple in the sense Was that how this log nitrogen feet can live and one more thing later it was found out that this oxygen is not the life of earth 59 planet, it is the feet of capta planet feet, so there is no such thing because there are many such logs which are living on earth 59.

Belonging, he has left even his world, that too because of his superpowers, many questions were troubling me inside me at the time, I could not understand what to do undefined tales what to ask because when I asked him about myself He didn't even tell me that I belong to some other planet, not a planet, why did he do this, and on the other hand, when the python collided, why couldn't any other planet go, because of the radiation of time protection? Why did only 59 feet hit. Somewhere behind it, there is no enmity between anyone and no one else If I have been missing for so many days, then Lucifer, Uncle Master Yang Lu and Bucky all have said is it okay, is Sapta Planet okay, where is all of them in some trouble and why are the logs calling me heart-wrenching, who is this? Credentials are the shadow of some existence, which is attached to me somewhere, I do not understand, after all, even after saying in then what can I do , I cannot stand it and make it stand out and when I became the protector of me and whenever I have I remember the past, so who is the right net why the energy of the wind bothers me, I remember the enough so much that I felt something different when the earth 59 feet came, the people here is not the same as their words , which is written in my own words and maybe these alphabets will give a new light to every hope to go ahead and tell the story of my part from which I was so different .

"

I HAVE
GOT CAUGHT
IN THE
PRAYERS
OF WHICH
PATHS
WHERE HATERD
HAS
GOT
ITS OWN
HEALTH
AND LOVE
HAS
ALSO
GOT
IT."

I was unaware of those people whose love was written only for love, why did lucifer uncle tell me that the logs of earth 59 are our enemies and why they were trained only in the thing and when for the first time the master one At the time of the session, did Earth 59 really attack us and if we did, why didn't we respond to them in return and if the people of Earth 59 Planet hate the people of capta Planet then why fallen love with me like in advertently? When did the right foot become their whole world, even without saying that why do people now look like me, why do I feel for the first time that every single thing that Lucifer Uncle had said to me is wrong. There is no existence and no foundation. The nib of one last question is bothering me even more that when will I remember those sari things, will I be able to survive earth 59 planet feet with the help of unfinished yaadis and finally the next day Who saved me and who? And if according to the time protection, if I was living in my past, then Earth 59 Planet ,And how in the future, he has come so far and why does this log Uncle Lucifer hate so much, after all what has he done to the people of Earth 59 Planet and this log why does he know the name of Lord of Blood Every foundation of my future is hidden in the illusion that even after seeing it, I can not attend to my charisma and why are these people hoping that I will save them from Lucifer Uncle, what is the reality of the world and this Why the earth planet people think about me as a kind of hero of the which save them fdrome the bad destruction by evil lords .

"I am forcely incaged inside the time
Otherwise they don't have a possession to incage me
But their love is so much fascinating over the time
Otherwise they will dump me"

II

NO WAY TO RUN

Day:145 (01ROHT)

Today I have spoken to fight such a battle in which even

if I lose, I will explain it to my own fate, I used to call Master Yang Lu Hamesah, who is my grandfather, or I came to know about this when I went in search of my canda ship because at that time my memories drom the past was reversible again and again ,Means 45% Covered Data When I set out to Earth59 to find my canda Ship, I found something that made me rejoice at the parts of my past that I used to explain my ruin. Means where dad started the experiment for the first time, I saw that lab, his feet were completely ruined and forged, when I disrespected him, I saw that like master one taught us, he was also in the invisible protocol. There was no such thing, it was a special that was completely closed outside, the foot was not even a scratch inside, in that time it was understood that it was a danger and then my powers were also not with me That's why I thought I should remove this body and find my spaceship because I have to go to my planet now , because so many secrets are connected between capta Planet and Earth59 Planet foot how I came to know that it is my dad's spaceship which I have never seen and no one has ever mentioned about it capta planet foot then how do I remember this spaceship and how do I know that dad had started this experiment and what experiment am I talking about, I was thinking of these things that in that time someone attacked me Whose face was neither like ours nor Earth 59 planet's people like the people of the earth 59 planet was scorched by radiation and a strange perfect glow was coming out of his eyes, due to which he could not even see him. He also had the Weakness Harlod's sword in his hands which only his race can use because Whee is his real hero. Weakness Harload's bad eyesight has saved us, he also told us that If there is one thing most powerful in the universe, it is the sword of Harlod and their army is even better than ours and their army alone can conquer the entire universe without Harload undefined.

> "**WICKEDNESS HARLOD** : *The king of such an elusive world, whose thinking and saying was only that theory of the father, who had created such a war create in which many innocent people had died, about Harload, the master had told us all that his trouble would ever happen. Neither can you nor you can try to make him die, nor can he ever die, only one thing can imprison him and maybe even murder him and that thing is nothing else - the powers of the mind which That was made by none other than my dad, whose suit has been made against P5 Platnium and not only that, he has the energy which can destroy any world, this world, in one stroke, human and all other creatures. Animals can tell them the way in a moment, the entire creation is annihilated, that foot is the only witness it deserves and can bear its power, which has talked about its past and future undefined*"

The Weakness that attacked me was none other than Harlod's only child Toxikant Suker It was many years ago when the Weakness Harlod attacked Earth59 and the capta Planet foot, when Master Yang Lu and Master and my Uncle Lucifer Weakness was imprisoned with the help of time protection, he could not imprison his children when my fight was going on with toxicant, so he was not feeling anything at the time, neither his powers nor the fight he taught by the master Wasn't able to fight him in protocol I don't know who the right energy was inside him when I was trying to move towards him it was trying to kill him happy time before I died my surgery energy was different It was probably my fault at the time because I had forgotten that my powers earth59 palnet legs did not work because time protection gave me double the attack of her har, not my past, against the external. Because of this I was unable to even stand my feet properly.

CONVERSATION

"***TOXICANT SUCKER** : Now your death is near human insects .*
***TYAG** : I don't think , I'm going to die so soon crappy gross ones .*
***TOXICANT SUCKER** : I'II even spare you if you dont't talk too much .*
***TYAG** : I don't think I even talk today if death is written then it is only yours .*"

Maybe my story could have ended in a bad day if Uncle Lucifer didn't come at the right time, he attacked me, man at the time, Lucifer Uncle saved me and as soon as Toxicant Sucker saw Lucifer Uncle he ran away why undefined Why is Lucifer Uncle Seh, such a mighty warrior of the universe afraid undefined

"

***TYAG** : Uncle Lucifer ,I cant't believe my feet that you are here .*
***UNCLE LUCIFER** : Tyag you are fine ,please stop let me help you ,your fears are filling too much .*

***TYAG** : How did you find me ? and all how : is capta planet foot .*
***UNCLE LUCIFER** : I'II tell you everything my kid let me heal you first .*
***TYAG** : I am so happy, seening you ,I can't tell how much I was missing you ."*

My life was saved for a few days, maybe a future accident was unknown to me, the dream that I saw was not turning into reality, I used to say that many times in the day I asked Uncle Lucifer about our planet and he logs Asked about feet he didn't tell me anything bash said so much that you won't go away from earth59 planet right now you are safe feet at that time so many such questions were tearing the walls of my face that after all Uncle Lucifer said to me that what we are doing for our planet , I asked him every time and he gave the same answer every time that nothing happened to him.

Keep your game happy day then my troubles increased even more when he was going back to seh then might wind attacked earth59 feet and his people leg also killed many innocent people many people became homeless from their home I did not understand these things that if no one attacked Earth 59 Planet foot in so many years, then I would Why do I say destroy the Earth59 planet as soon as I come and where people consider me to be a hero, I can't do anything for them even after saying nothing, why I do not have my powers and Uncle Lucifer did not tell anything and before him I don't know how to help my people. I don't know how to help them.

Jeffrey is such a warrior who was one of the best commander of Sapta Planet and probably no one will know this because I have never mentioned about him, he says no log can forget your accidents, you can forget your love. By the way, Jeffrey and I have grown up together since childhood, feet were much better than me, so he had to leave the sapta planet long ago to protect the time protection, and the day my Kanda ship crashed after hitting the back of the asteroids Geoffrey Why was gone the public was neither me nor did she ever mention her feet, her fiber stone locket said everything happy time, the day I came to my senses that the public could never forget me, foot master another master Yang Lu told us all the time.

I have been taught that if you want to move forward in life, then take time and effort with you and take your feelings away from yourself, your humanity will never let him go away, if you say so, then you will never let him go on your path.

If you can't separate it, then why the practice of walking towards it, which is your weakness, no one else can know better than you, in the whole world and what is your reality, no one can know it better than you Whoever one sided victory is the best warrior in the world and at this time he doesn't need any destination, he should say that enough self-confidence, on which he can trust and move forward. Out of the two, we get the training of only one, so trust yourself in the journey.

No other creature can move you, only your rudeness can move you forward, there is no such gift of your body which can set a destination without it, it was not such a thing that we could not love and could not live together. Further love is like keeping only one thing, at that time neither such futures were uploaded in my system, nor did I have the honor that I can do this, maybe my true is incomplete, I will tell you the whole truth at the feet. I had come to my senses, I saw the fiber stone near me, I could not digest the male thing in the male time, I could not understand these batis, because only one energy was attracting me towards it. My friends were costing me a poison, because I used to say to do everything, my feet were not right at the time, that they should choose those paths to whom they have no need to go, I never thought that Jeffrey and my meeting will be very special, that too in such a trouble which we both were unaware that earth59 used to say in the laws of planet I called Jeffrey the next time with the help of Fiber Stone so nothing happened to him undefined

CONVERSATION

"

TYAG : *Hey ,if you are listening to me then i need your help to escape earth59 ,that too from might wind evil .*

JEFRRY : *Tyag how are you ? you are right ,aren't you ?*

TYAG : *I'm fine and I know capta planet is in danger but I need your help ,can you help me ?*

JEFRRY : *Why are you saying this ,yes I definitely help you .*

TYAG : *Thanks alot .*"

Legs were not a matter of real danger at all because the powers of the megahat wind were not so much that they could destroy the entire earth planet. But he was not weak nor his powers, because before that, when Lucifer had defeated him, he had made him tied, feet he had somehow escaped from the capta planet, feet who is this Might Wind?

> "***MIGHT WIND*** *: Talked long ago, when there was a place named Halle which was very close to Earth59 and capta Planet, it was ruled by humans who, in appearance like us, their feet could control the entire universe and destroy it. And his chieftain was none other than Might, he had found such a wonderful thing like Lords of Time Protection that could destroy this plant in one stroke, he misused it, he used those powers with the help of Lords of Time. Tried to die of protection only because he said that time and the entire universe should rule the feet. K Log tried to convert into faith and was successful. Legs At the last minute, the wind freed itself from our grave by any means undefined*"

He was known in the whole universe by the name of the god of anger, who would go into someone's fear and take his anger away from him and then to destroy his anger, he would separate every part of it, he has known so much that he has no one. Countless feet that scoundrel is released again today and I do not think that earth 59 planet foot has come for some purpose, foot shish bar he is not going to survive. I still don't understand this thing that if they knew that I am earth 59 feet then why didn't they come to pick me up and why am I being kept away from my planet if my memories can't get back then maybe I could never know the truth that who is my child after all He had already healed before growing up and that time Uncle Lucifer tried to leave before that time. had come and he also asked me to leave that house soon and the spaceship in which my dad's many experiments and pasts were hidden he also made me sick why undefined The more my story is progressing, the more the question increases I have been thinking of these lamps that at the time of Earth59 planet Earth, Might Wind attacked it and before it tried to kill many people, we were standing in front of the human demon.

CONVERSATION

MIGHT WIND : Oh both of you are the heroes of earth 59 planet ,I may not be lost anywhere ,children by looking at you .

TYAG : If these children do not become the reason for your death ,then die protecting yourself ,demon .

MIGHT WIND : Sorry but I am very disappointed to hear the sound of my death (laughing).

TYAG : So be ready to accept it .

When we got into a fight with Might Wind then , we already knew that we would never be able to win with him. I felt right at the time, my powers were not with me, she was hoping that I could completely protect my people and I did the wrong time when the light wind attacked my rude feet, then my fear Legs have come a long way, which were happening in a short time, neither Might Wind could understand this, nor did I understand this thing, Jeffery had already said this to Mighat Wind. The demon of the body grew to his death, as soon as he attacked me again, his surgery powers got absorbed in me, he did not know this at all. I was surprised in the sense that I was not able to understand that how can she also die so soon, it is not possible because it is not possible.

Lucifer Uncle, no one can kill in this shish universe because he himself is a soul sucker, so how can I take his angry feet captive?

Jeffrey fainted for a while trying to make sense of me because the energy I was feeling was a kind of energy that I had never felt, it was so powerful that it blew my breath with a single punch. When did this happen undefined means who is the right energy in me that I am unable to maintain, after all who are these right friends who stay in my mind and seek help from me, what has happened to me.

“

MANY
SECRETS
HAVE BEEN
MADE
IN THE
GIFT OF
WAR,
MANY
CROWNS
HAVE BEEN
MADE
IN THE
GIFT OF
LOVED
ONES

AND THE
BLESSINGS
OF WORDS
ARE STILL
THERE
TO ACHIEVE
FATE
FEET
FEEL
BUT
NOW
THE
SITUATION
HAS
CHANGED
TO
GO
TO THE
GATHERING OF
OTHERS ."

III

FAMILY UNCONDITIONAL SEPERATION

A person's thinking can be wrong, even his attitude can be wrong, feet a person can never be wrong Can't feel he has his own thoughts, he has his own thoughts and he also has a love Remembering that I try to count my every moment, which I have forgotten, so maybe my love also returns Our attitude also recommends to be separated from us A person can try to forget his worries if he is not his feet If he is his then he can never erase it from his charity enough tries to remember him all the time He also makes each of his passers-by lane close to the ravine, he never loses his feet He conspires, he can never get away from him Well why am I saying these baton, maybe the reason for this will be known soon. It was because a lot of people already knew this thing that I am nobody else's mind, how did they know this? When I probably went close to my dad's spaceship and at the time when my fight was toxic, how did he know that I am in my mind, because the day I came to know about this, maybe I was not in his time because when I killed Might Wind, so I had lost some time Didn't see it, when I had fainted, then for the first time I met my dad, he felt that he is alive feet, were all those visions true, were I? my dad was really alive i also saw the spaceship where he was in making mind and saw lucifer uncle also with him for a long time and mom too was moving on my feet like a dream i saw every wonderful thing in the universe Look, to get who the log is killing each other, I saw the reality of every human being of Sapta Planet and also the childhood memories which were completely different as everyone had told feet are my dreams true, this is the reality of what they have told me At that time I could not understand anything because at that time I was seeing so many visions that I could not control them. I never asked to see those visions and never told them to try to lane closer to me because I knew the truth, probably not completely because when Lucifer Uncle told me these words that your dad How did he die? They were what they had made for me, this sapta planet was because neither father belonged to them nor mother belonged to them, and it is a matter of mind that the one whose mind is made between the past and the future, that no one else made them my father.

my dad didn't say at all that the powers of our mind were in the wrong hands because at that time he had many such people and demons from the pain universe behind him, so dad used to tell those powers to be bashful, maybe this thing to me too Happy day it came to know that dad was not a normal person at all because the way he had created our mind, it could have happened only if those eight naib ruths of the universe were with him. And those eight naib ruths belong to the same family only We could have made the mind pure, what was the need to make the feet, how did dad make it, after all how can someone's sacrifice save humanity and even if he is innocent, after all, dad made it, then for whom did he make it? , what danger they had felt long ago, which was to come in future. He who never let me feel that he was not in my own world now, even though I did not have the family to fight, after all Witness took my whole world China, that too for such a thing which has no value. Why am I saying these things and who has made me happy with my surgery in China, who is that witness after all, who is equally in love and hate when I was looking at all the visions. See the thing which is true, I never call it manna in my feet I am not talking about my lucifer uncle, who killed my dad, that too only for the poor man, whom dad used to tell him to hand over his feet who was the right bailout because of which lucifer uncle killed dad and showed me such dreams that even after thinking of him, he hates himself now. Recommend to do the feet who consider them so close to them as their entire family, why did they betray this undefined which pharaoh's pond was that they killed their own friend and I am their son's son Why is love expressed like this? After all, what is the reality of their undefined

I knew this thing that why Lucifer uncle had killed my dad, I do not know at all, in which secret, my loved ones' yards were burning in the pyre, I did not even know in the bailout what happened after all. Between them I saw all the visions well before he killed my dad undefined

Conversation

"***LUCIFER*** *: You have to walk with me right now that too capta planet foot .*

TYAG *: I can't go anywhere with you .*

LUCIFER *: What ?*

LUCIFER *: Renunication you earth59 are not safe .*

TYAG *: So how can I stay safe with the murderer who killed my dad ?*

LUCIFER *: Oh ! so you just found out that I kill your dad , so now its your turn .*"

If there was death on some part of the day, then maybe I would have adopted it because the habit was lost, I had lost the habit of showing off. The beginning had to be the beginning of the leg, when Lucifer meant the blood sucker did not know this at all, now I have the powers of the mind, the ones I was fighting in my feet, he was the biggest warrior of the universe, he had such powers that I had The weak can also kill me, because my mind chose me, I did not choose her, man time and fear is protected only when his anger is with him The bailout of my fear, with the help of which I tried to fight many times, I lost my leg many times when victory was behind the death but it was in my part because my love played such a trick, because of which death was in my destiny then not my leg I have found my place to begin with, my feet have ended?

"I am upset because of myself
why to blame others
I found myself safe in the arms of them but
they cheat me
why to blame others
I found exhausted myself
why to blame others
I have ruined my whole life for myself
why to blame to others"

Ending Of Hero

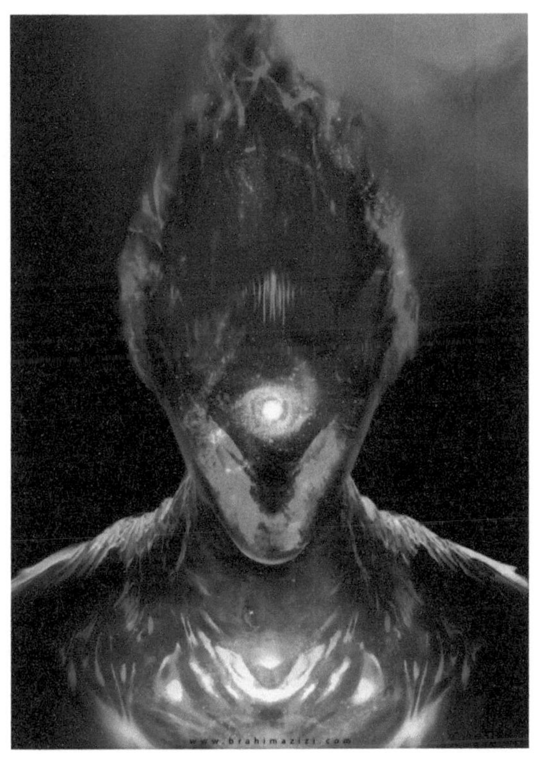

9 798887 041834

Printed by Libri Plureos GmbH in Hamburg,
Germany